READ THE BOOK, LEMMINGS!

Written by **Ame Dyckman**

Illustrated by **Zachariah OHora**

L B

LITTLE, BROWN AND COMPANY
NEW YORK   BOSTON

Foxy found a quiet spot
to read his book
about lemmings.
"Huh!" Foxy said.
"Says here,
lemmings *don't* jump off cliffs."

JUMP?
I'LL JUMP!

ME TOO!

DITTO!

said a
lemming.

said a
second.

said a
third.

"Huh!" said Captain PB.
"Guess they didn't read the book."
Foxy looked.

Foxy sighed. "Sir?" he asked. "May I borrow your bucket?"

"Fine," said Captain PB. "But your lemmings better not eat my fish."

Foxy pulled.

Foxy dumped.

Foxy gave his lemmings names—and hats—so he could scold them properly.

"Focus, Jumper!" Foxy said. "You too, Me Too! Ditto...Ditto."

Foxy opened
his book.

READ THE
BOOK,
LEMMINGS!

"Huh!" said the lemmings.
"Exactly!" Foxy said.
"The book says you *don't*."
"Don't?" asked Jumper.
"Don't what?"
"Jump off cliffs,"
Foxy said.

JUMP?
I'LL JUMP! said Jumper.

ME TOO! said Me Too.

DITTO! said Ditto.

Foxy groaned. "I hate to ask again...."
"Oh, take it!" grumbled Captain PB.
"My fish already taste like lemmings!"

WHAT WERE YOU THINKING?

Foxy yelled.
"The book says you *don't* j—"
Foxy stopped.
"Just read the book,
lemmings."

AHHHHHHHHHH!

said the lemmings.

They took a look and
returned the book.

"Huh!" said Captain PB.
"Good thing you didn't
say 'jump'!"

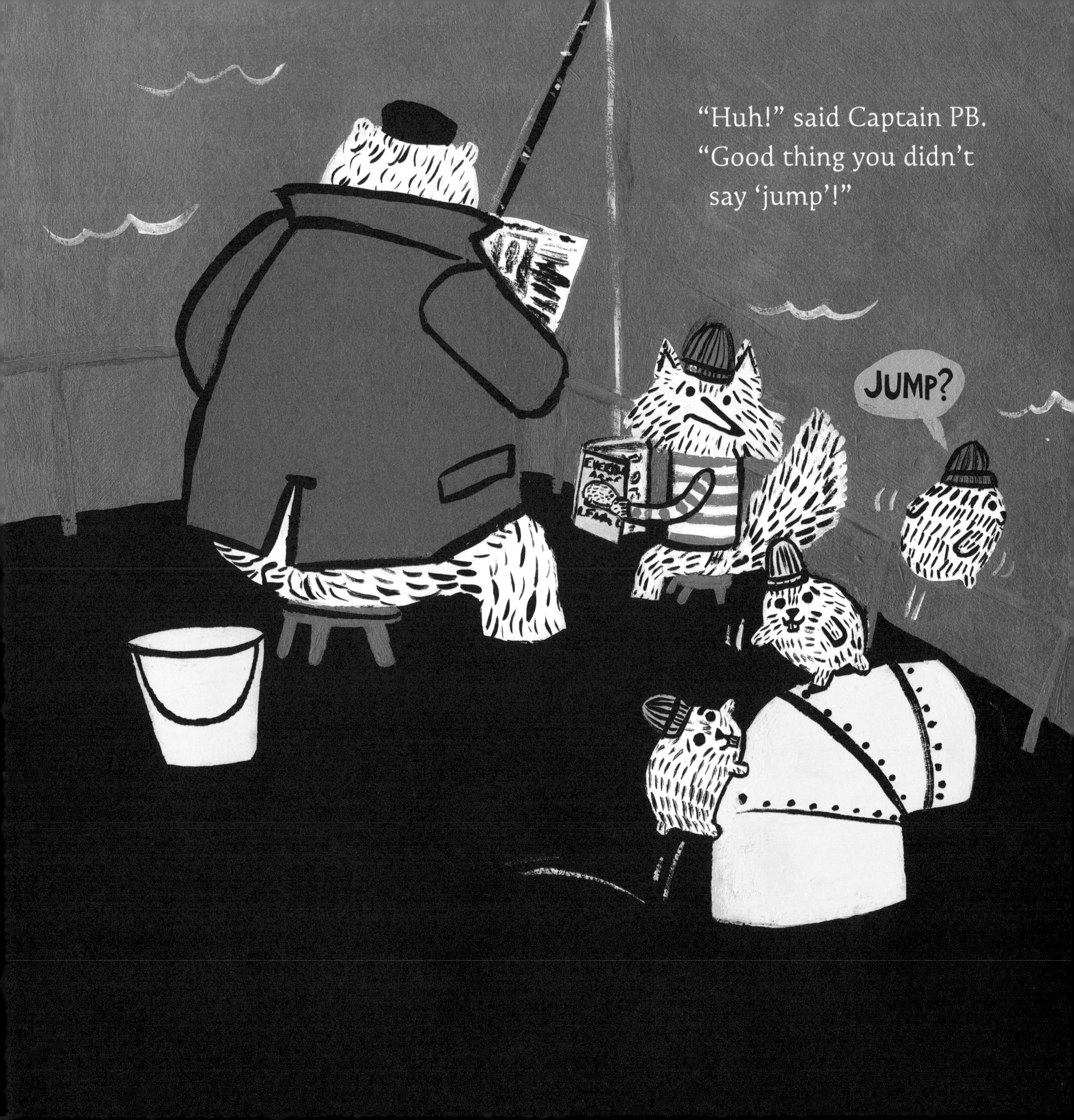

GERONIMO-O

"Nope!" said Captain PB.
"They definitely didn't
read the book!"

There was no time to use the bucket.
"Watch my book," Foxy said.

Foxy scooped.

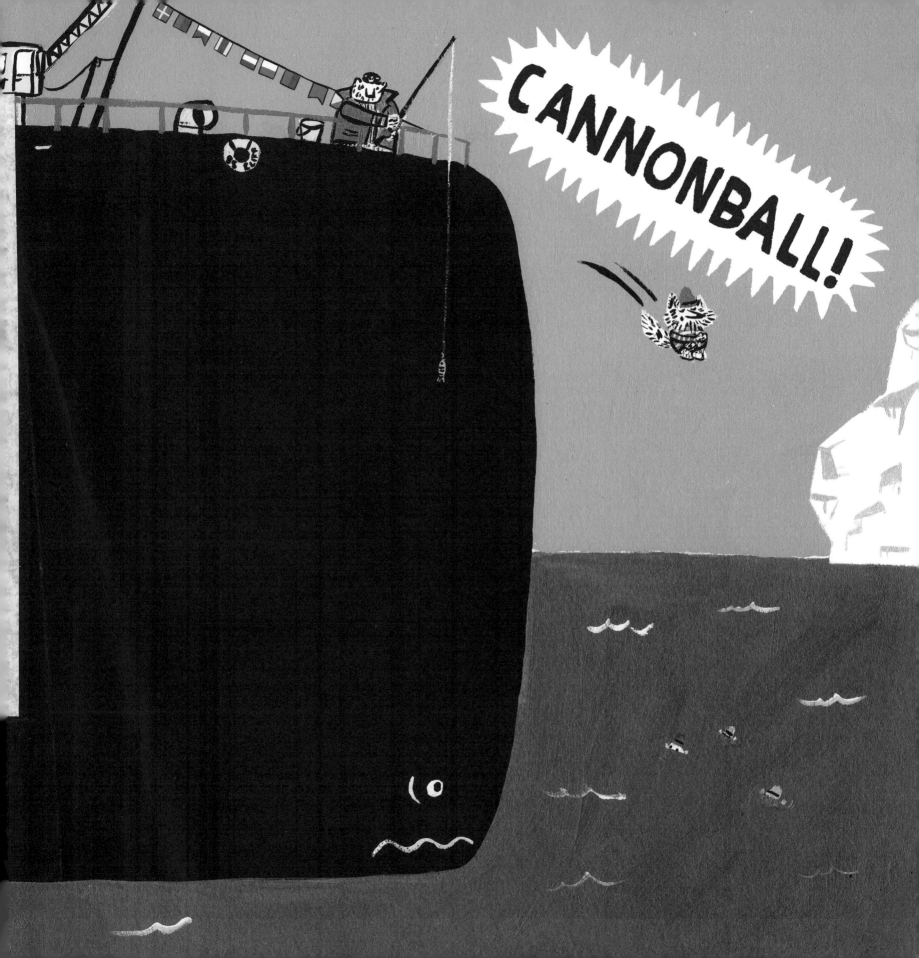

Foxy swam.

Foxy flopped.

Foxy blinked.

"Huh!" said Captain PB.
"That's a good start!"

"I'll teach you to read, lemmings,"
Foxy promised.

They practiced reading all afternoon.

Foxy finally returned to his reading.
But Captain PB could not.

Where's my paper?

EVERYTHING ABOUT LEMMING

For Zach. I'll always jump at the chance to work with you.
—A. D.

For Ame. This is just the tip of the iceberg.
—Z. O.

Author's Note:

When I was little, I saw a movie that showed lemmings jumping off cliffs. Years later, I learned that, except in very rare cases, lemmings DON'T jump off cliffs. My first thought was, "OH NO! DID ANYONE TELL THE LEMMINGS?!"
So, we made this book. You're welcome, lemmings.

This book was edited by Mary-Kate Gaudet and designed by Saho Fujii and Aram Kim. The production was supervised by Erika Schwartz, and the production editor was Marisa Finkelstein. This book was printed on Gold Sun woodfree. The text was set in Galena, and the display type was Potato Cut and hand-lettered. The illustrations in this book were painted in acrylic on 90-pound acid-free Stonehedge paper.